Martha

the (imaginative)

Mouse

written and illustrated by Karen Lang

Canadian Cataloguing in Publication Data | Lang, Karen | Martha the Mouse
Hardcover Edition: ISBN 978-0-9812948-1-0
Softcover Edition: ISBN 978-0-9812948-3-4
Printed and bound in Canada by Debbie Tait & Associates

Design | Ringleader Graphics Management

Acknowledgments – I would particularly like to acknowledge and thank my husband
Don, who has so enthusiastically encouraged me in the writing, illustrating and
publishing of this book, and for his absolute support in all my artistic endeavors.

I would also like to sincerely thank the many friends and family members who very
generously and insightfully provided encouragement, feedback and editing wisdom…
my parents Bob and Bunny Skelly, my aunt Myrtle Mandeno, Thais and Gary Turner,
Nora Spence, Heather Coons, Heather Godden, Gail Singer, Tiina Adams, Rosemary
Lindsay, Michelle Campbell, Mary Richardson, Cathy Abbott, Janet Newlands, Martha
Coles, Barbara Klunder, Sheila Casgrain, Julie Sharpe, Audry Mah, Debbie McNair,
Natasha Laluque, Nancy Eisenhauer, Gerry Moore, and of course my children, Erin,
Robyn, Tim and Trevor…..always inspiring. Again, if I have inadvertently forgotten
anyone,… I am not worrying about it… I have a strategy for managing that… and a
good imagination….

www.marthathemouse.ca

This book is for my children, Erin, Robyn, Timothy and Trevor,
whose childhood journeys provided such an infinite source
of enjoyment and wisdom.

Imagination unlocks the possibilities.

Martha the Mouse wanted to be

A good many things as you will soon see.

But try as she might, despite all her wanting,

It was not very easy, and in fact somewhat daunting.

She dreamed of adventure, glamour and dance,

Being smart and creative...
and NOT just by chance.

But luckily, Martha discovered the key.
She could be who she wanted, ultimately.

Pretend!

Imagine!

How simple is that?

Throw on a costume!
Slap on a hat!

Tutus and top hats, baubles and chains,
Glamorous glasses, wigs and long manes.
Plastic nose and mustache of all shapes and sizes,

A good dress-up box has endless surprises

A pirate could take her on many adventures,
On far away seas and in search of great treasures.

The eye patch and sword made her daring and bold,
And a tiny bit wild if the truth should be told.

Playing a teacher felt clever and grand

In front of the class
with pointer in hand

She taught with flamboyance, drama and flare.

And by end of the day was slumped in the chair.

Now dancing on stage
in front of a crowd
Was TOTALLY scary,
stressful and loud.
But as soon as
she pulled on
pink tutu and tights.

She danced and spun circles late in to the nights.

Donning a police hat and badge with a shine
This clever detective could help solve the crime
And when cases got complex, solutions so near,...

It was donuts and coffee that helped her think clear.

To investigate stories, to tell a tall tale

She sorted through clues and followed the trail.

Writer? Reporter? No one came close
To the imaginative stories that Martha could boast.

An artist with attitude pondering a scene,

She could be ANYTHING she EVER might dream.
Until...

There came a dilemma of such a grand scale,

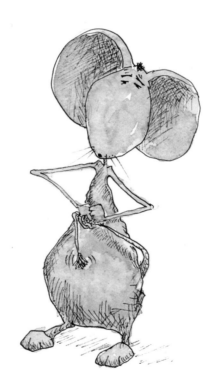

...She pondered a moment untangling her tail...

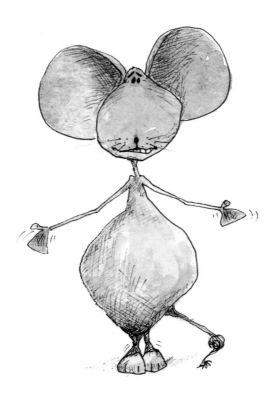

How could she be all these things "just like that!"??
Without the help of a costume or hat??

What would happen for instance, if caught unaware
Not a costume or prop to pull out of the air?
Could she be who she wanted with drama and flair?

Like ideas that come to you out of the blue,
Martha thought for a moment and then she just knew!

Pretend!

Imagine!

Costume or NOT....

She could be who she wanted!!
.....Imagine that thought!!!

While the dress up box had the makings for fun,

Martha herself was the creative one!

And Martha discovered, as you can now see,

Just how imaginative she really could be.